WITHDRAWN

Fairy Handbook

Handbook Series

© 2010 Cuento de Luz SL
Calle Claveles 10
Urb. Monteclaro
Pozuelo de Alarcon
28223 Madrid, Spain
www.cuentodeluz.com

Text and illustrations © Monica Carretero
English translation by Jon Brokenbrow

ISBN: 978-84-937814-9-1
DL: M-47436-2010

Printed by Graficas AGA in Madrid, Spain,
November 2010, print number 65691

Text and illustrations:
Monica Carretero

Fairy Handbook

CUENTO
DE LUZ

Do fairies exist?
Where do they live?
How many of them are there?
Can you see them?

Have you ever walked through the
countryside and heard the leaves
rustle and seen them move,
but when you went over to look,
there was nothing there?

Are there days when you look at yourself in the mirror and you think you look really pretty? Do you often go to bed and feel deliciously sleepy, and lay there with a smile on your lips?

Are they days when you're studying and everything seems easier? Do you remember afternoons with your friends when you've had a really great time?

If you answered 'yes' to nearly all these questions,
then you're ready to enter the world of the Fairies,
where everything is magical and different:
where nothing is impossible,
where everything is a beautiful as the stars,
and danger appears in mysterious ways.

Do fairies exist?

Yes!!
Yes!!!
Yes!!!!
Yes!!!!!
Yes!!

Hang on, hang on, just a minute! I'd like to bring a bit of mystery into this Fairy Handbook. If you all come charging in like that, you'll ruin my plans. I'll ask you all again. Do fairies exist? The answer is a definite, energetic, resounding and unquestionable

Yes.

Sit down, make yourself comfortable,
take a deep breath and get ready,
because you've just entered the real world of the fairies

The origin of the Fairies

Legend tells that one afternoon, a fortune-teller's daughter went out for a walk in the countryside. As she was strolling along, she saw the most beautiful butterfly there ever was.

The little girl fell in love with the butterfly, and the butterfly fell in love with the little girl. They were never apart.

Then one day, the butterfly died. The little girl cried and cried as she held it in her hands, until she fell asleep. When she woke up, she discovered that two large wings were covering her little body. The fortune-teller's daughter had become a Fairy.

The same thing had happened at the same time, in the same instant, in different parts of the world. Hundreds of Fairies had been born.

Fairies from around the world

Here you can find some fairies that live on our planet.
They are spread out all over the world.

Eskimo

American

English

Russian

Oriental

Mexican

Argentinean

Senegalese

Spanish

French

German

How to spot a Fairy

They are incredibly delicate creatures.

They have pretty faces, and their enormous eyes can see the future.

Fairies are between 2 and 4 inches high. They have small bodies, and their arms and legs are much longer and slimmer than a person's. Don't forget that they're half girl and half insect! They blush easily, and they always wear fresh flowers to perfume their hair.

Also, they have really big feet, but don't ask me why. And finally, to see them fly is a sight for sore eyes, as they gracefully swoop and flutter. It really is amazing. When you see a Fairy, you want to be her best friend, you want to kiss her and hug her, make her little dresses, and never be apart from her...
It's precisely for that reason that take great care not to be seen.

The Fairy and her wings

The differences between the different types of fairies are
what make them so extraordinary. For example,
the number of wings they have, which makes
them fly in different ways.

Two-winged fairy

They fly like birds over fields
and cities. They rise and fall
with incredible grace.

One-winged fairy

They move like fish when they fly,
close to the ground.

Three-winged fairy
They fly in a slightly wobbly,
zigzagging way.

Four-winged fairy
There's nothing more stunning than
to see these fairies flying in a group.
They seem to dance, with all of their movements
perfectly coordinated, and will leave you with
your mouth hanging open.

Where do fairies live?
City fairies

There are fairies all around us, but not everyone can see them.
In the city, there's so much hustle and bustle that there's hardly
any time to look at what's going on around us.
Can you find the eleven fairies in this street?

Bakery

Country fairies

In the countryside, life has a different rhythm. The sun comes up, and some fairies are having hot pollen for breakfast, others are doing complicated yoga exercises, and others are still fast asleep.

Nomad fairies

There
are some
fairies who are
great travelers. They
don't like living in the same place
all the time, and move from place to place
with their homes on their backs. Here are two examples
of the houses they carry with them as they travel around the world:

The shell house and the wheeled house.
They're really handy, as you're always
close to your bed or the bathroom.

A meeting place for fairies

Fairies love to meet up to chat about their lives
and share their experiences.
The Fairy Mansion is the
best place to do it:
it's big, pretty and in
an unknown country
far, far away.

The Fairies' festival calendar

The longest day: celebrated on the 21st of June.
The fairies prepare all sorts of delicious food and fresh orange juice.
They sing and dance until the sun goes down.

The coldest day: celebrated on the day the first snowflake falls.
The fairies put on their woolly hats, their scarves and their gloves,
and throw snowballs at each other: Kapow!

The tenth full moon: celebrated on the night of the tenth full moon.
All of the fairies meet under a large sequoia tree, where they tell
stories and perform plays.

The flower festival: celebrated on the 21st of March, when the
flowers begin to appear all over the countryside. The fairies wear
their best dresses and put flowers in their hair, and dance the whole
day long.

The falling of the leaves: celebrated on the 22nd of September.
The fairies fly high into the sky holding hands, and look at the lovely
colors of the leaves on the trees before they all disappear.

The longest night: celebrated on the 7th of December.
This is the night when the fairies do most of their magic.
Then they meet at the Fairy Mansion and prepare an
amazing breakfast.

The fairies always find reasons to have parties, but these are the six days when they have their biggest festivals: in the open countryside, under the stars and amongst the flowers. What great fun!

Fairies you might know

The Muddled Fairy

You go to put on a dress and it's got a stain, you go to eat some chocolate and someone's eaten it, everything's a jumble, nothing's as it should be today.

The Busy Fairy

Making the bed, folding the clothes, laying the table and drying the glasses. What a lot of work!

The Giggly Fairy

Ha, ha, ha!
Hee hee hee!
Ha, ha, ha!
Hee hee hee!
What a silly attack of the
giggles! You can't stop!
Enjoy yourself, who cares!

The Scatter-
brained Fairy

Goodness me,
what a disaster!
Instead of getting on
the bus to take you home,
you've ended up in the zoo.

You bump into these fairies all the time.
They live with you, but you can't see them.

The Huggy Fairy

When she's nearby
you just want to
be hugged and loved.
You're feeling very cuddly
and snuggly.

The Kissy-Kissy Fairy

Kisses to the left,
kisses to the right,
pecks on the cheek
and big smackeroos.
What a lot of kisses!

The Hideaway Fairy

You've lost something and you can't find it, but you're sure it was right next to your bed... are you going crazy? No, the Hideaway Fairy is here, so watch out!

The Nutty Fairy

Today you're feeling really wild, and you can't stop doing crazy things. What's up with that little girl? Simple: the Nutty Fairy's in town.

The Bubbly Fairy

You're so happy today, running, jumping and dancing all over the place. It's great to have the Bubbly Fairy around: I'm in such a good mood!

The Grumpy Fairy

Everything's wrong today, everything's a drag, and all you want to do is complain. Get out of here, Grumpy Fairy! All you do is make me want to scream!

The Gloomy Fairy

Sometimes you want to cry, but don't know why. You just want to be alone. Don't worry, you just bumped into the Gloomy Fairy and she'll soon be gone.

The Brainy Fairy

What a brain! That's one smart cookie! When the Brainy Fairy touches you with her wand, learning's as easy as pie.

Now you know them, you can see them

Whenever you lose something...
whenever you get an attack of the giggles and can't stop....
whenever you're having a sad day and you don't Know why...
when you feel so happy you just want to bounce around the room...
when you're feeling Kissy and cuddly...

That's when the fairies are right there
with you, when they're fluttering around
your head, when they're whispering
magic words to you and filling
your life with enchantment.

Fairy Activities
Wordsearch

Find six fairies that you have seen in the book.
You can read them from top to bottom or from left to right

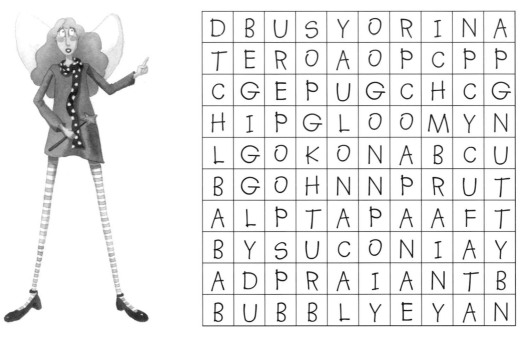

D	B	U	S	Y	O	R	I	N	A
T	E	R	O	A	O	P	C	P	P
C	G	E	P	U	G	C	H	C	G
H	I	P	G	L	O	O	M	Y	N
L	G	O	K	O	N	A	B	C	U
B	G	O	H	N	N	P	R	U	T
A	L	P	T	A	P	A	A	F	T
B	Y	S	U	C	O	N	I	A	Y
A	D	P	R	A	I	A	N	T	B
B	U	B	B	L	Y	E	Y	A	N

Solution: Busy, Giggly, Nutty, Gloomy, Bubbly, Brainy

Recipe for Fairies
Chocolate and strawberry bonbons

(Ingredients for you and three friends)

24 strawberries • One big bar of chocolate • Half a glass of milk • 24 wooden skewers

Melt the chocolate and the milk together in a microwave for 4 minutes.
Skewer the strawberries and dip them into the hot chocolate. Leave them to
cool in the fridge for an hour. A delicious, refreshing treat!
In winter, eat them when the chocolate's still hot.

Find the seven differences

Find the seven differences between the pictures.

Solution: Stone, star on the magic wand, the number 2, stripy curtain, black boot, flower on dress and Fairy's hand

Riddle

It flies and it isn't a bird. It's got wings and it isn't a mosquito. What is it?

Answer: A Fairy